This book belongs to:

_____

For Dave

This paperback edition first published
in 2013 by Andersen Press Ltd.,
20 Vauxhall Bridge Road,
London SW1V 2SA.
Published in Australia by
Random House Australia Pty.,
Level 3, 100 Pacific Highway,
North Sydney, NSW 2060.

10   9   8   7   6   5   4   3   2   1

British Library Cataloguing in Publication Data available.

ISBN 978 1 84939 793 3

red sledge

LITA JUDGE

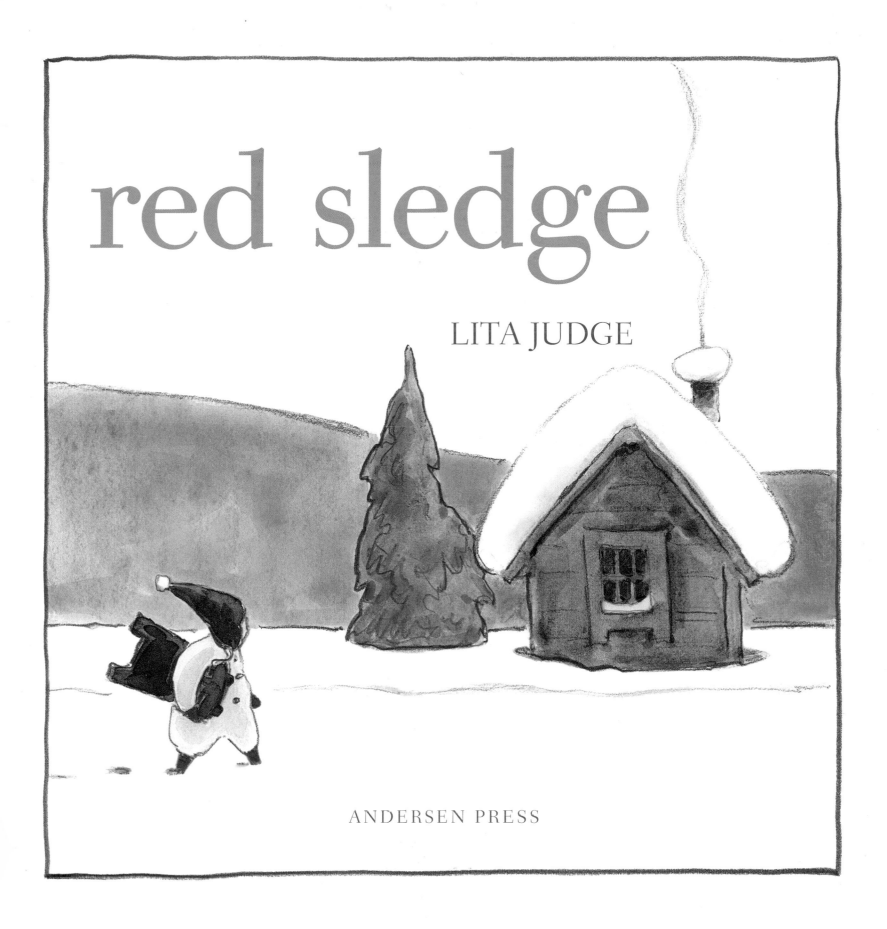

ANDERSEN PRESS

Scrinch scrunch scrinch scrunch scrinch scrunch

Scrunch scrinch **scrunch scrinch scrunch scrinch**

eeeeeeee
ooooo
eoeoee

Alley-oop

ssssssffft

Scrinch scrunch scrinch scrunch scrinch scrunch

The End

Other books you might enjoy:

9780862649982

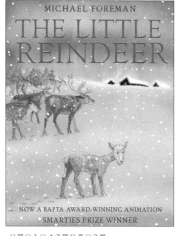

9781842705827

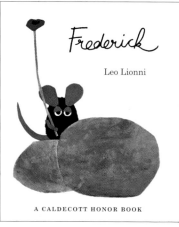

9781849395182

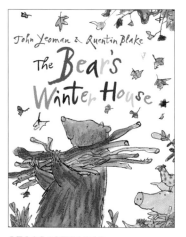

9781842701960

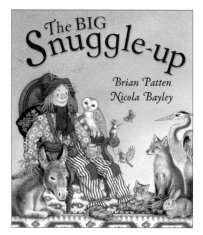

9781849394666

9781849393096